THE LITTLEST DRAGON
GETS THE GIGGLES

Collins
YELLOW
STORYBOOK

THE LITTLEST
DRAGON GETS
THE GIGGLES

by Margaret Ryan

Illustrated by Jamie Smith

CollinsChildren'sBooks

An imprint of HarperCollinsPublishers

For Jonathan, with love

First published in Great Britain by Collins in 1997
Collins is an imprint of HarperCollins *Publishers* Ltd
77-85 Fulham Palace Road, Hammersmith,
London, W6 8JB

3 5 7 9 8 6 4 2

Text copyright © Margaret Ryan 1997
Illustrations © Jamie Smith 1997

ISBN HB 0 00 185678 2
ISBN PB 0 00 675292 6

The author and illustrator assert the moral right
to be identified as the author and illustrator of the work.

Printed and bound in Great Britain by
Caledonian International Book Manufacturing Ltd,
Glasgow G64

CONTENTS

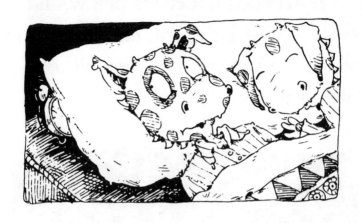

THE LITTLEST DRAGON
GETS THE GIGGLES

It was very early morning.
In the dragons' cave ten dragons lay
fast asleep. Suddenly, the pillow of
Number Ten, the littlest dragon,
began to ring. TING! TING! TING!

"Shush… not so loud," whispered
the littlest dragon, blinking open his
eyes. "Don't wake the others."

He reached under his pillow and switched off his alarm clock. Then he slipped out of bed and tiptoed to the big cave kitchen.

"Today I'm going to be first for breakfast," he said. "I'm fed up always being last. By the time I get my breakfast the tea's cold, the toast's soggy and somebody else has pinched the plastic frog from the cornflake packet."

The littlest dragon climbed up onto
a stool at the sink and made his tea
with water from the hot tap – he
wasn't allowed to boil the kettle yet.

He popped his bread in the toaster and was just reaching for the cornflakes when a big dragon paw swiped the box from him.

"Oh good, a new box of cornflakes," said his big dragon brother, Number One. "My turn to get the plastic frog."

"When is it MY turn?" asked the littlest dragon.

"Oh great, tea's made," said big brothers Two, Three and Four, pouring themselves some.

"That's MY tea," said the littlest dragon.

"Toast's made too," said twin
brothers Five and Six, catching the
slices as they popped out of the
toaster.

"And that's MY toast," said the
littlest dragon.

But the other dragons paid no heed.

The littlest dragon quickly sat
down at the big kitchen table and
tried to get some breakfast. He was
just reaching for the tea when...

"Shove along, Number Ten," said brothers Seven and Eight. "We need more space."

The littlest dragon wiggled along the bench and was just reaching for the toast when...

"Move along, Number Ten," said brothers One and Two. "We need more room."

The littlest dragon wiggled along the bench a bit more and was just reaching for the cornflake packet when...

"Shift your bum, Number Ten," said brother Number Nine, rather rudely, and pushed the littlest dragon so hard that he fell right off the end of the bench onto the floor.

The littlest dragon stood up and rubbed his knee.

"This won't do," he muttered. "This won't do at all. I set my alarm clock for extra early, and I still haven't had any breakfast."

Then he had his first idea.

He went to the kitchen window and peeped outside.

"Oh look," he said in an innocent little voice. "I think I see the postman coming with a big parcel for us. And I think it says on it SWEETS FOR THE DRAGON BROTHERS FROM GREAT AUNT GEORGINA."

"Great," yelled brothers One and Two. "Hope there are some sticky lollies."

"And chocolate toffees," said Three and Four.

"We like jelly babies," said Five and Six.

"We like everything," said Seven, Eight and Nine.

The kitchen cups rattled as nine
dragon brothers thundered towards
the door.

The littlest dragon gave a smile and a sigh and sat down at the big kitchen table. At last he had it all to himself.

But not for long.

Soon the other nine dragons
were back.

"It's not the postman at all,"
said Number Four.

"There was nobody there,"
said Number Seven.

"You must be seeing things,
Number Ten," said twin brothers
Five and Six.

"Mmmm," said Number Ten, but that soon changed to "OW" as the other nine dragon brothers piled back onto the bench and pushed the littlest dragon off the end.

· The littlest dragon stood up and rubbed his elbow.

"This won't do," he muttered. "This won't do at all."

Then he had his second idea.

He went to the kitchen door and peeped outside.

"Listen," he said in an innocent little voice. "I think I can hear the ice cream van coming."

"Great," yelled brothers One and Two. "Hope it's got some mint choc chip."

"And strawberry with nuts," said Three and Four.

"We like dribbly chocolate," said twin brothers Five and Six.

"We like everything," said Seven, Eight and Nine.

The kitchen plates rattled as nine dragon brothers thundered towards the door.

The littlest dragon gave a smile and a sigh and settled down at the big kitchen table. At last he had it all to himself.

But not for long.

Soon the other nine dragons were back.

"It's not the ice cream van at all," said Number One.

"There's nobody there," said Number Two.

"You must be HEARING things, Number Ten," said twin brothers Five and Six.

"Mmmm," said Number Ten, but that soon changed to "OW" as the other nine dragon brothers piled back onto the bench and pushed the littlest dragon off the end.

The littlest dragon stood up and rubbed his behind.

"This won't do," he muttered.

"This won't do at all."

Then he had his third idea.

If he couldn't get any breakfast sitting AT the table, perhaps he could get some standing ON the table.

The littlest dragon climbed up onto the big kitchen table and was just reaching for the tea when...

"Move along there, Number Ten, you've got your tail in the milk."

The littlest dragon moved along and was just reaching for the toast when...

"Move along there, Number Ten, you've got your tail in my tea."

The littlest dragon moved along
and was just reaching for the
cornflakes when...

"Move along there, Number Ten,
you've got your feet in the butter."

The littlest dragon moved along
and – WHOOSH – his buttery feet
skidded along the table and –
CRASH – he fell off the end.

He lay there on the floor,
wondering which bit of him to rub
first, when he noticed all the dragons'
feet and tails. Then he had his fourth
and best idea.

He crawled away into the hall and opened up the big cupboard where the odds and ends were kept. He searched about till he found two long pieces of hairy string and a fluffy feather duster.

"This should do the trick," he said.

He crawled back under the kitchen table and carefully tied the feet of one dragon to the tail of another. Then, he tickled all the dragons' feet with the fluffy feather duster.

"Help, help, who's tickling my feet?"

"Oh no, I can't stand it."

"Tee hee, tee hee, stop stop!"

But the littlest dragon didn't stop till all the laughing dragons had fallen over onto the floor.

"Whose leg is this?"

"Give me back my tail."

"I've got three legs!"

The littlest dragon laughed and sat down at the big kitchen table. At last he had it all to himself. He poured himself some tea, buttered himself some toast, and opened a new box of cornflakes. Now it was his turn to get the plastic frog.

Then he started to eat his breakfast, but – HEE HEE HEE – he had to stop because – HO HO HO – looking at all the laughing dragons – HA HA HA – wriggling on the floor – TEE HEE HEE – gave him a fit of the – TEE HEE HEE HO HA HA – giggles.

"TEE HEE HEE HO HA HA!"

A VERY HOT DAY

It was a very hot day.
In the dragons' cave the ten dragon
brothers were getting ready to go to
the swimming pool.

"Who's pinched my special racing swimming trunks?" said Number One.

"Not me," said the littlest dragon. "They're too shiny."

"Who's pinched my special racing goggles?" said Number Two.

"Not me," said the littlest dragon. "They're too scary."

"Who's pinched our special racing nose clips?" said twin brothers Five and Six.

"Not me," said the littlest dragon. "I *like* water up my nose. It tickles."

Nine dragon brothers pulled on their special racing swimming trunks, then wrapped their goggles and nose clips in their towels and put them in their sports bags. Number Ten didn't. He pulled on his baggy bermudas then searched round for his towel.

"Who's pinched my special
Number Ten towel?"

"Not me," said Number One. "It's
far too small for me."

"You never use it anyway, Number Ten," said Number Two. "You always shake yourself dry."

"But I need it to wrap my arm bands in," said the littlest dragon.

"No, you don't. You're not coming to the pool with us," said Number Seven.

"Why not?" gasped the littlest dragon.

"Because we're playing races in the big pool, and you can only go in the baby pool," said Number Eight.

"Because you're still too little," laughed Number Nine.

"I AM NOT," yelled the littlest dragon, standing on his tiptoes and stretching himself up as far as he could go.

"Oh yes you are," laughed his
nine big brothers and went off
without him.

"BYE BYEE!"

"It's not fair," muttered the littlest dragon, stomping into the big cave kitchen. "I always get left out. Just because I'm the littlest."

"What's not fair, Number Ten?" asked his mum, who was making a special chocolate mud pie for tea.

"It's not fair that the others get to go swimming and I don't. Just because I'm too little to play races in the big pool. Could you take me swimming, Mum?"

"Sorry, Number Ten," said his mum, "but I really have to finish making this mud pie. Great Aunt Georgina is coming to tea."

That gave the littlest dragon his first idea.

He went to the big hall cupboard where the odds and ends were kept and found his red plastic bucket.

Then he ran out into the garden and filled it right up to the top with oozy, squidgy mud. He brought it inside and up-ended it on the kitchen table.

"There you are, Mum," he said, "a perfect mud pie for Great Aunt Georgina. Now can we go swimming?"

"That's not exactly the kind of mud pie I had in mind, Number Ten," sighed his mum. "My mud pie's not made with real mud."

The littlest dragon trailed out
into the garden again and went to see
his dad who was weeding the flower
beds.

"Hullo, Number Ten," said his
dad. "All alone?"

"The others have gone swimming
and left me behind. It's not fair. Just
because I'm too little to play races in
the big pool... Could you take me
swimming, Dad?"

"Sorry, Number Ten," said his
dad, "but I really have to finish
weeding these flower beds. I want
them looking nice for Great Aunt
Georgina when she comes to tea."

That gave the littlest dragon his
second idea.

He rushed back into the house,
opened up the big hall cupboard
where the odds and ends were kept
and got out his red plastic spade.

Then he went back into the garden and started weeding one of the flower beds.

When he had finished he gathered up all the weeds to show his dad.

"Look, Dad, I've dug out all the weeds for you. Now can we go swimming?"

"Those aren't weeds, Number Ten," sighed his dad. "Those are flowers you've dug up. You've left in all the weeds."

The littlest dragon was just trailing back into the house when...
HONK HONK HONK
SCREECH SCREECH SCREECH

Great Aunt Georgina skidded up to the cave in her supersonic dragmobile. She stepped out of the car wearing her very best flowery frock and hat.

That gave the littlest dragon his
third idea.

He ran over to Great Aunt
Georgina and gave her the flowers.

"Hullo, Great Aunt Georgina.
These are for you. I know how much
you like flowers, and they match your
hat. There's only Mum and Dad and
me here just now, all the others have
gone swimming. I wanted to go too
but they said I was too little, and
Mum and Dad are too busy getting
things ready for you to take me."

"Oh dear," said Great Aunt Georgina. "What a pity." Then she smiled, "I have an idea, Number Ten. Would you like me to take you swimming?"

"What a good idea," said Number Ten in an innocent little voice. "Now why didn't I think of that?"

He climbed into Great Aunt Georgina's dragmobile and they roared off with a loud honking of horns and screeching of tyres.

When they got to the swimming pool they found the other nine dragons standing outside, looking miserable.

"What's the matter?" said the littlest dragon. "Why aren't you inside playing races?"

"We can't get in," said Number
One.

"There's a special swimming gala
on," said Number Two.

"There's no public swimming today," said Number Four.

"Except in the baby pool," said twins Five and Six. "And we're too big."

"What a shame," smiled the littlest dragon. "But I'm going to swim in the baby pool. You can come and watch me if you like."

They all went inside. The other nine dragons and Great Aunt Georgina sat and watched while the littlest dragon splashed and played in the baby pool. He had a great time floating on the rafts, chasing the stripy beach balls and riding on the plastic dolphins.

"Watch me! Watch me!" he yelled.

"We're watching," muttered his nine big brothers.

Finally, Great Aunt Georgina's tummy gave a loud rumble. "I think it's time we went home for that chocolate mud pie," she said.

She called over to the littlest dragon,
"Time to come out of the pool,
Number Ten."

"Okay," said the littlest dragon
and climbed out.

The nine big dragon brothers
looked at each other in horror. Too
late they fumbled in their sports bags.
Too late they found their swimming
towels. Too late they threw them to
the littlest dragon.

Too late because, as usual, the littlest dragon just shook himself dry.

"PPPPPPPPPPRRRRRRRRRRRPP!"

Nine big dragon brothers and one
great aunt got soaked.

"Oops, sorry," giggled the littlest
dragon. "Good thing it's a very hot
day."